IMAGINE THAT

Licensed exclusively to Imagine That Publishing Ltd
Tide Mill Way, Woodbridge, Suffolk, IP12 1AP, UK
www.imaginethat.com
Copyright © 2019 Imagine That Group Ltd
All rights reserved
2 4 6 8 9 7 5 3
Manufactured in China

Written by Oakley Graham
Illustrated by Jennie Poh

ISBN 978-1-78700-072-8

A catalogue record for this book is available from the British Library

For Bodhi - OG

Bubble Trouble

Written by Oakley Graham
Illustrated by Jennie Poh

Bodhi loves bath time and what he loves most about bath time is ... bubbles!

But the bubbles never last long enough for Bodhi.

One day, Bodhi decided to add some extra bubble bath when his mum wasn't looking.

He couldn't wait to get into the bath and play with the bubbles until his feet and fingers went wrinkly!

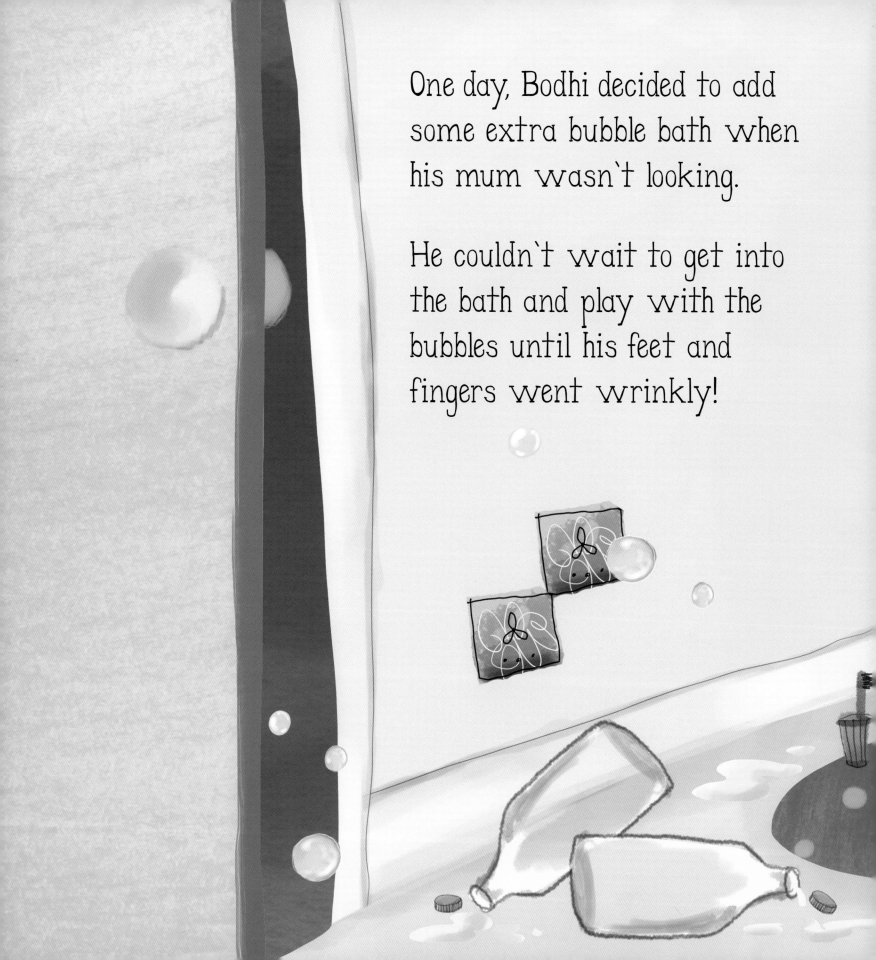

As the bubbles began to form under the tap, Bodhi giggled. The bubbles that were filling the bath weren't like ordinary bubbles – they were enormous!

The bubbles got **bigger** and **bigger** and **bigger!**

Soon the bubbles filled the bathtub,

and then the bathroom,

and then the landing,

and then the entire house and garden!

Bodhi was busy thinking what to do next when he felt a strange floaty feeling in his tummy. There were too many bubbles to see, but Bodhi felt as if he was riding on a rollercoaster at a funfair.

When the bubbles finally cleared, Bodhi discovered that he wasn`t in the bathroom any more ... he was floating along the street, trapped inside an enormous bubble!

At first Bodhi was a little bit scared,
but soon he began to enjoy the floaty feeling.

Bodhi floated over big cities ...

and wild oceans.

He soared across dry deserts ...

and bounced over enormous sand dunes.

He whooshed over noisy jungles, waving to the monkeys down below ...

and soared high above giant mountains.

The people that Bodhi floated past
could not believe their eyes!

Floating around the world in a bubble was lots of fun, but there was a problem ... Bodhi was getting hungry – very hungry indeed!

Bodhi had to find a way to get home!

Then Bodhi had a brilliant idea!

He started to use his arms and legs to steer the giant bubble, just like his hamster steered its ball back at home.

The bubble travelled back over giant mountains, over noisy jungles, across dry deserts, and over wild oceans and big cities.

Bodhi steered the giant bubble all the way home, through the front door, up the stairs and into the bathroom where it rested on a bar of soap.

Luckily, Bodhi's mum came into the bathroom just as the soap made the bubble pop and she caught him in her arms.

'That's enough bubble trouble out of you for one day!'
said Bodhi's mum, giving him an enormous hug.